KNOCK, KNOCK!
Who's There?

For Keith
—S.G.

A DRAGONFLY BOOK PUBLISHED BY ALFRED A. KNOPF, INC.
Text copyright © 1985 by Sally Grindley
Illustrations copyright © 1985 by Anthony Browne

Manufactured in Great Britain   10 9 8 7 6 5 4 3 2 1

Library of Congress Cataloging-in-Publication Data
Grindley, Sally. Knock, knock! Who's there?
Summary: All sorts of scary creatures knock on the door and ask to be let in, but the
door only opens for Daddy, who comes in with hot chocolate, ready to tell a story.
[1. Father and child—Fiction] I. Browne, Anthony,   ill.   II. Title.
PZ7.G88446Kn   1986   [E]   86-112
ISBN 0-394-88400-0   ISBN 0-394-98400-5 (lib. bdg.)   ISBN 0-679-81385-3 (pbk.)

KNOCK, KNOCK!
Who's There?

by Sally Grindley

Illustrated by Anthony Browne

DRAGONFLY BOOKS · ALFRED A. KNOPF
New York

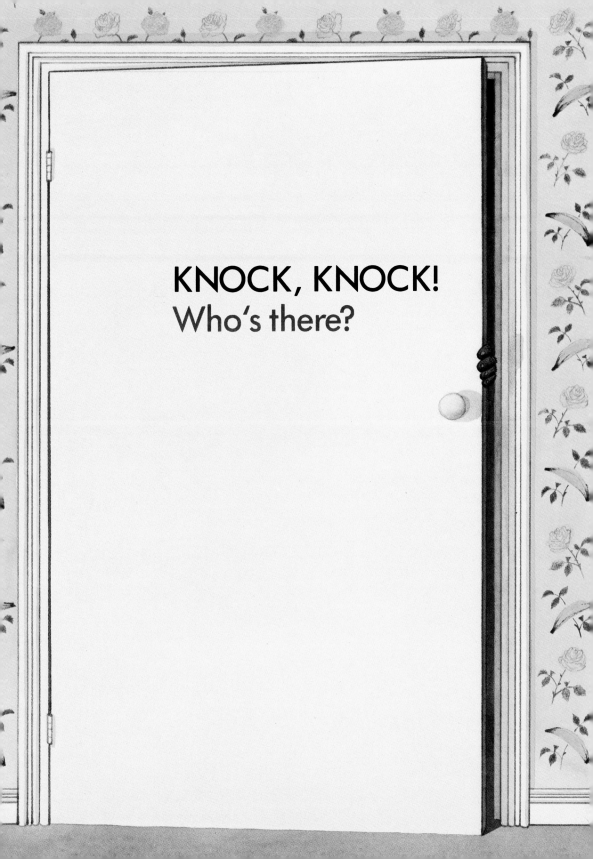

KNOCK, KNOCK!
Who's there?

I'm a great big GORILLA
with fat furry arms
and huge white teeth.

When you let me in,
I'm going to hug your breath away!

Then I WON'T let you in!

KNOCK, KNOCK!
Who's there?

I'm a wicked old WITCH
with a long pointed hat
and a wand full of magic.

When you let me in,
I'm going to turn you into a frog!

Then I WON'T let you in!

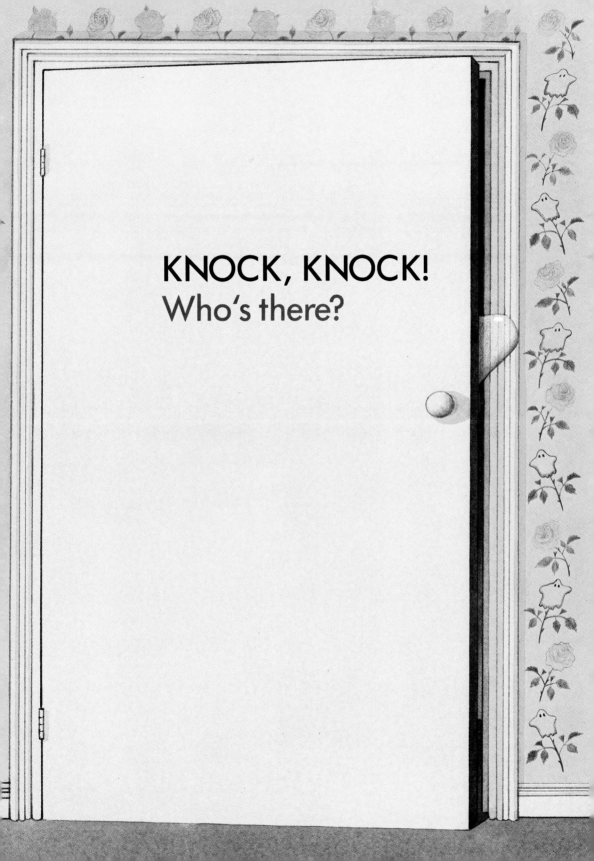

KNOCK, KNOCK!
Who's there?

I'm a very creepy GHOST
with a face as white as a sheet
and chains that jangle and clank.

When you let me in,
I'm going to spook you!

Then I WON'T let you in!

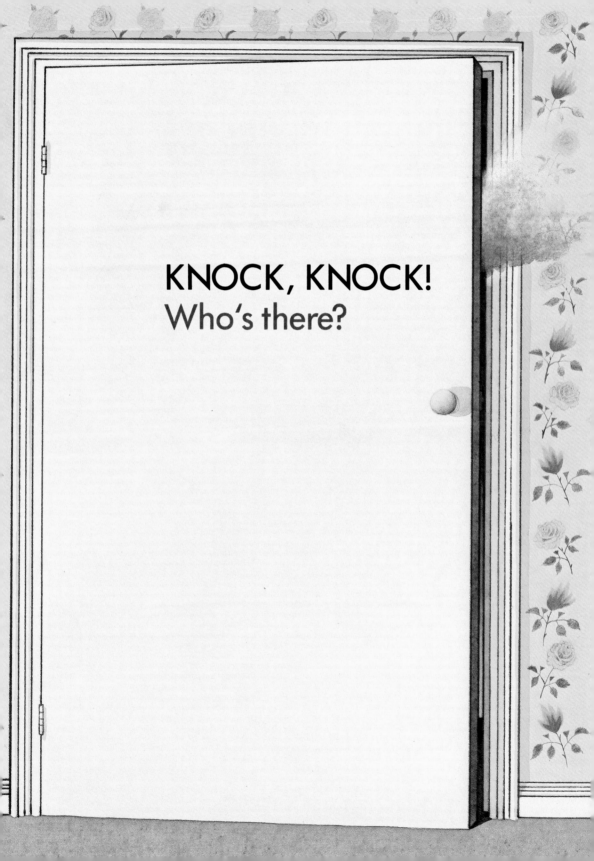

KNOCK, KNOCK!
Who's there?

I'm a fierce scaly DRAGON
with smoke up my nose
and fire in my mouth.

When you let me in,
I'm going to cook you for my dinner!

Then I WON'T let you in!

KNOCK, KNOCK!
Who's there?

I'm the world's tallest GIANT
with eyes like footballs
and feet like football fields.

When you let me in,
I'm going to stomp on you!

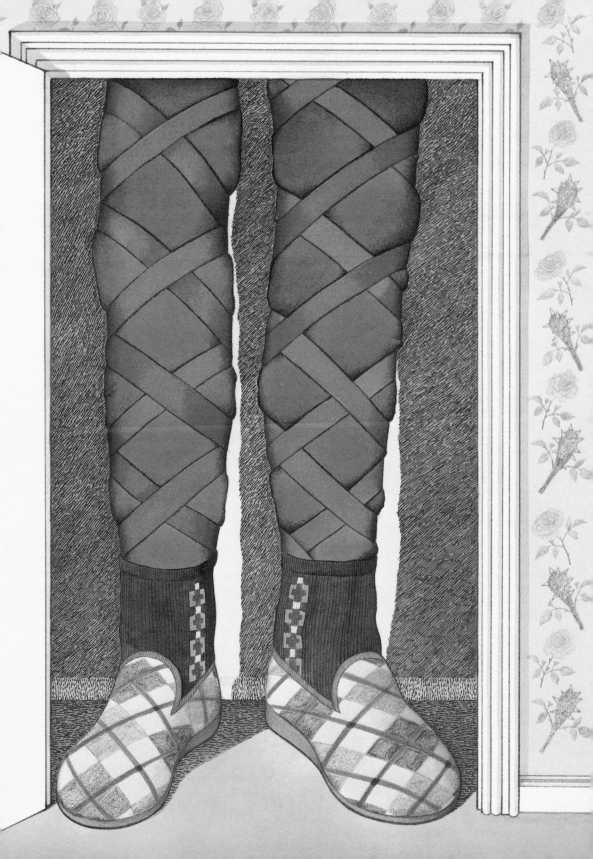

Then I WON'T let you in!

KNOCK, KNOCK!
Who's there?

I'm your big cuddly daddy
with a mug of hot chocolate
and a story to tell.

PLEASE may I come in?

COME IN, COME IN, COME IN!

There was a gorilla at the door,
and a witch
and a ghost
and a dragon
and a giant
and ...

I knew it was really YOU!